SERIES

Refuge Cove

Lesley Choyce

ORCA

orca soundings

ORCA BOOK PUBLISHERS

National Library of Canada Cataloguing in Publication Data

Choyce, Lesley, 1951-

Refuge Cove

(Orca soundings)

ISBN 1-55143-246-3

I. Title. II. Series.

PS8555.H668R43 2002   C813'.6   C2002-910694-X

PR9199.3.C497R43 2002

First published in the United States, 2002

Library of Congress Control Number: 2002107486

Summary: When Greg discovers a family of refugees in a lifeboat off the rugged coast of Newfoundland, he risks everything to help them.

Orca Book Publishers gratefully acknowledges the support for its publishing programs provided by the following agencies: the Government of Canada through the Book Publishing Industry Development Program (BPIDP), the Canada Council for the Arts, and the British Columbia Arts Council.

Cover design: Christine Toller
Cover photography: MaxXimages
Printed and bound in Canada

08 07 06 05 • 7 6 5 4 3

IN CANADA:
Orca Book Publishers
PO Box 5626, Station B
Victoria, BC Canada
V8R 6S4

IN THE UNITED STATES:
Orca Book Publishers
PO Box 468
Custer, WA USA
98240-0468

For Norma and Sonny and Gordy

LC

Chapter One

Our house was half on, half off the land. It was jammed into the side of a rocky hill and part of the house was standing on stilts, stuck out over the water. It was the weirdest house I'd ever seen. Alongside was parked the car. And on the roof rack was my thirteen-foot Laser sailboat.

I can usually get the little boat off the roof of the car by myself. But when I heard the voice I was flat on the ground, pinned by my boat.

"Funny way to sail a boat," he said, not offering to help. "Around here, a fella usually puts the boat in the water and then gets in. Don't think she'll work upside down like that on dry land."

The guy must have been at least seventy years old. I don't think he'd shaved a day in his life. He had that foreign-sounding accent that all the people around here have.

"I nearly broke my back. How about a hand?" I hated it when adults tried to be cute. This guy thought he was funny.

"All you had to do was ask," he said, sounding a little hurt. "Mainlanders do funny things. How was I to know that this wasn't your idea of a good time?"

He didn't say another word. He lifted the boat and helped me carry it down to the water of the cove. Then he sat down and watched as I got the rest of the gear, slipped in the centerboard, fitted the rudder and rigged the sail.

"Some toy," he finally said.

"No toy," I countered. "This is a precision machine. And you're looking at a sailing champion." It's true, I had won races on Lake Ontario, lots of races. I was one of the best.

"But that's no boat for the North Atlantic. This here's an ocean, lad, not some inland lake."

"Right," I said, feeling the sting of his insult like a slap in the face. "Thanks for the advice." This was my first big chance to get in the water and rip. All I had to do was get out of the cove and into the sea beyond. I could see from the whitecaps that there would be a good wind.

My mother and I had only been in Newfoundland for four days. It wasn't anything like Toronto at all. But that was why we had moved here.

It was the dream they both had — my mom and dad — back before my father died. We would sell everything, pack up and move to a little outport like this on the coast a million miles from anywhere.

Now we had made the big move, just the two of us. Deep Cove was home. But it wasn't like a dream come true at all. It was pretty weird. My mom was really upset about every little thing. I was still trying to hold things together. My trick was this: I didn't think about my father. Instead, I'd concentrate on sailing, on the races I'd won back in Ontario and what it felt like to keep pushing my little Laser to the absolute limit.

Today was the day I'd finally get my sailboat into the Atlantic. Today was the day I'd see just how far I could push.

Looking towards the cove entrance, I started to push off but I was snagged. I turned back around to see that the old guy had grabbed the back of the boat. He had a stern look on his face. I think I had left a bad impression. "Don't go out too far. I'm serious. I'll be out after I get some tea. That's my boat over there." He pointed to an old beat-up fishing boat with a small cabin. "By the way, I'm Harold."

Looks like a pile of junk, I almost said. "I'm Greg," I said.

"A couple of boats of refugees came in down the shore. Dropped off by a big ship, left to float around in a little lifeboat not much bigger than your toy here, Greggie. Some folks say there might be more coming ashore. That's why I'm going out for a look later. You keep your eyes open too."

"Sure," I said, wanting to get under way. Refugees in lifeboats weren't my problem. "And don't worry about me, man," I said, banging on the sleek fiberglass hull. "You wouldn't be able to catch up with me. I'll be flying."

Trying not to smile, Harold gave me an icy stare. He picked up my floater jacket. "You forgot this," he said.

I shoved it back to him. "I don't need it," I said. "I push the limits but I never go down."

"Where are you from anyway?" he asked as I pushed off.

"Toronto," I answered, not turning around to look at him.

"Figures," I heard him say as I picked up a quick little puff of air and tacked for the entrance of the cove.

As soon as I was past the final cliff of the headland, I felt the wind fill my sail and we keeled far over. I held hard onto the rope and leaned way out over the water. The speed was amazing. It was like we had just been injected with rocket fuel. I let out a howl and jumped up to stand on the edge of the sailboat and lean even further out over the water. It was all I could do to keep the centerboard and rudder in the water. Man, we were flying! I had so much salt spray in my eyes I could hardly see. But what the hell, it was a big ocean. I had lots of room to maneuver.

And then, through the tears from the wind and the salt spray, I saw something that really freaked me out. It was dead ahead. It was blue and white and was the size of a large building. It took a couple of seconds to register. I was staring at a freaking iceberg.

I came about hard and let the sail rattle a bit in the wind. "I love this place," I said out loud. The morning sun made the blue ice look electric. I slid in so close that I was in the shadow of this monster. Looking back at where I'd come from, I saw that I was already a long way from land.

But no way was I just going to sit there and gawk. I needed action and I needed speed. I pulled around so the wind tightened the sail with a hard slap. I slipped over to the other side of the boat, grabbed onto the rope and let the wind send me flying.

I could just barely keep us from going over, but I'd been around Lasers for a long time. I knew how to control things in any wind. My instincts were sharp as a razor.

But I guess the rest of my brain was fast asleep. What I should have realized was that where there are monster-size icebergs, there's bound to be baby icebergs as well.

And I learned that fact the second I heard a large *whump* and went hurtling through the air, directly into the sail and over into the freezing cold water. I came up spouting seawater and shocked at the cold. The boat was on its side in the water. I had run into an ice cube the size of a Toyota. I swore at myself but wasted no time. I hopped on the centerboard and jumped up and down until the boat came upright.

I was soaking wet and freezing when I crawled back in. A quick look at the sail told me I was in deep trouble. It had a long gash where I had been thrown into it. I took a quick look behind me and saw the coastline was far away.

Chapter Two

You can't sink a Laser, but you sure can freeze your butt in one. I tried jury-rigging the sail, but it only ripped further. So I wrapped myself in it and watched the shoreline. I tossed in the swells, waiting for a miracle.

My fingers and toes were numb, and my head was throbbing by the time I saw a dark dot appear in the distance. After a few minutes, it was clear that it was a boat and it was zigzagging in my direction.

I yelled and screamed until I was hoarse. When I could see it was truly a boat heading towards me, I let the ripped yellow-and-blue sail out to flap in the wind so I might be seen.

It seemed like a year went by, but finally the boat pulled alongside. It was Harold. He threw me a rope. I could barely grab on, my hands were so stiff with cold.

When the boats bumped, Harold reached over and helped me on board. "You dead or alive?" he asked. "I can't tell 'cause you look like a ghost."

"It was an accident," I said, brushing off his question. "Could have happened to any-one. You could have told me about the ice." I should have been grateful, but for some reason I was feeling humiliated.

"Get in the cabin. Warm up. Pour some tea."

I didn't say another word. I ducked into the low little cabin. My toes began to thaw and my fingers began to move. Harold walked in just as I started to cry.

He took one look at me and acted like it

was no big deal that I was crying. "It's all salt water, boy. The sea, the stuff that flows in your veins, those tears. We're all full of salt water."

I needed to explain why I was crying. It wasn't the fact that I'd screwed up and nearly died. It was something else. "My father died last year. Heart attack. He just died." That was why I was crying. I missed him that much.

Harold seemed a little confused. Then he poured me a second hot cup of tea and put it in my hands. "I know exactly how you feel," he said. "My old man died just last year, too."

I looked up at him, puzzled. "How old was he?"

"Ninety-one."

I thought that this was some kind of joke. My father had just turned forty. "It's not the same," I insisted.

Harold took a big gulp of tea right from the pot and shook his head. "Nope. You're wrong. It is the same. I know exactly how you feel." He got up and went back to steer us into Deep Cove.

Mom made me take a hot shower. "You want me to call a doctor?" she asked.

"No." I felt more embarrassed than anything. Here I was supposed to be the man of the family and I end up giving my mother more to worry about.

She let out a sigh. "I guess nothing is quite turning out as planned. First your father. Then the move. Now this. Greg, what are we doing here? Maybe we shouldn't have gone through with it. This is all different. We were supposed to move down here with your father and live happily ever after."

My mom was a dreamer. So was my old man. They had wanted to quit what they called "the rat race," take the money they saved and live in a remote outport by the sea. Me? I just wanted to live anywhere there was water and wind.

"We're out of the rat race," I consoled her. "You should have seen this iceberg," I told her. "It was beautiful. I've never seen anything like it."

"But you didn't have to run into it," she

said and lit up into a smile that let me know everything was going to be okay.

Just then, the door burst open. Harold, over six feet tall and looking a bit like a deranged criminal, walked into the house. I thought my mom was going to scream.

"It's okay, Mom," I said. "This is Harold."

Harold just tilted his head. "Got a decent sewing machine?" he asked.

"What?" my mother asked, flabbergasted.

Harold held up my torn sail. "I checked the boat. It's okay. No cracks. Looks solid. Sail's got a few problems, though."

"Who are you?" my mother now screamed at him.

"Name's Harold, like the boy said."

"He found me and brought me back," I said.

"Oh." My mother relaxed a little. She still seemed unsettled. "I guess I should thank you," she said. I could tell she didn't trust this stranger. "You scared the living daylights out of me. Why didn't you knock?"

Harold shrugged. "Don't know. Never

thought of it, I guess. Folks knock before they come in in Toronto?"

Right then I was glad I had met Harold. And not just because he had helped me out on the water. Mom and I needed all the friends we could find.

"Got a sewing machine?" Harold asked again. "I'm good at this. The best there is. I'll only charge you my standard fee."

"Which is?" my mother asked.

"Which is nothing."

My mom smiled, warming up to this crazy old coot. "I'm not sure we'll be needing the sail, though. I don't think it's safe out there for Greg. Not with icebergs and God knows what."

I figured she was going to say something like that. But if that was what she wanted, we would have to move back to Toronto. I couldn't live anywhere without sailing.

"Mom?"

"I'm sorry. I just can't stand to lose you too."

"I know what you're saying," Harold

began. "But I think the boy just made a mistake today he'll never make again. He picked the wrong day and he didn't know what to look out for. We all make mistakes. A different wind direction and a sharp eye for little bergers and he'll do just fine."

I don't think my mom was convinced. But as hulking Harold sat down at my mom's Singer sewing machine, she found it so comical that she cracked up laughing and couldn't say another word.

Chapter Three

My sail looked pretty lame with a big white patch down the middle, but it worked. While my mom watched, I tacked back and forth around Deep Cove with my floater jacket on. It wasn't exactly exciting, but it was good to be on the water.

People from Deep Cove kept showing up at our house to give us food — their way of welcoming us to their community. My mom could never quite get used to them walking in without knocking so she put up a little sign that said, "Please knock before entering." But everyone ignored it.

Harold took me out fishing in his boat. "Maybe we'll catch some fish, maybe not." We never did get our lines wet, but he showed me some monster icebergs and he showed me how to avoid the smaller "bergers" and "berger bits."

"Another boat of refugees came in down at Harrington yesterday. They nearly drowned coming ashore."

"Where are they from?" I asked as we came in close to a craggy jumble of rock that he called Boink Island.

"Asia somewhere."

"Why are they coming here?"

"I guess because it's a good place to sneak ashore and not get caught. But it's not a safe coast unless you know it."

"Ever get in trouble out here?"

"Lots of times. Especially when I was running rum. Had to do it in the fog sometimes."

"You were a smuggler?"

"Was. A long time ago. Made lots of money. Got in lots of trouble. It was the time of my life."

It wasn't until a couple of weeks later, in the middle of June, that I got to go out in my Laser again. Harold had taught me everything he could from the deck of his boat. We had surveyed every inch of coastline for miles.

"Wanna come along for the cruise?" I asked him.

"Big man, little boat. I don't think I'd fit. Besides, I'd only get in the way and slow down a hotshot like you."

It wasn't a mega-wind, but a good stiff breeze was blowing off the land when I steered a course out beyond the cove. My mom was home painting rooms and feeling pretty good. I told her I'd be careful.

I stood up on the gunwales and let the boat fly with the wind. I toured a couple of bergs and kept my eyes peeled for every cube of ice that bobbed. The world was blue, blue, blue. Sky, sea and everything in between. I wanted my life to stay like this forever. I felt free and alive.

Off in the distance, I spotted a couple of whales spouting. That really blew me away. They were too far away for me to give chase, but I decided to keep watching for more and try to get in close for a good look. Twenty minutes later, I spied something maybe a mile further out and to my left. I came about in the wind and headed straight for it.

Soon it became clear that it wasn't a whale at all. It was a boat, a pretty small boat — no cabin, no sail. As I came closer, it seemed that there was no one aboard. It was just an empty lifeboat that must have been cut adrift from some ship. Curiosity got the better of me. I decided to go up real close for a look.

There was a tarp over the top of the boat. I tied a rope onto her and let my sail luff in the wind. With all Harold's talk about rum smuggling, I think I half expected that I'd lift the tarp and see a boatload of drugs or smuggled gold or booze or something.

I undid a knotted rope holding down one corner and thought I'd just take a peek. Suddenly, a knife came jabbing up right through the tarp and nearly sliced off my left nostril. I screamed and fell back into my Laser. As the tarp flapped open I saw a dark-skinned man with a crazed look in his eye jump out. The knife in his hand was aimed at my throat.

We were rocking around like we were ready to dump. All I could think was that I was in over my head again. The guy had one hand tight on my throat and I was pinned down. The other hand held the knife. He was snarling at me but I couldn't make out anything. Then I looked in his eyes and noticed that he was as scared as I was. He was breathing hard and he was trying to say something. "You tell, I kill," was what I finally made out.

"I won't tell, I won't tell," I said, not knowing what he was talking about.

The guy eased up a little, but he looked like a firecracker about to go off. Just then the boom of my sail came whipping around in the wind. I yelled, "Duck," and I pulled him down. He got the wrong idea and lunged at me with the knife, slicing into my arm.

I let out a wail at the pain and fell back onto the tiller. I think I scared him because he suddenly dropped the knife. He scrambled for it in the bottom of the boat. He was about to lunge at me again when I heard another voice.

A girl had come out from under the tarp in the other boat. She was yelling something at the man. I don't know what. I was ready to jump overboard to get out of the way of the knife. I kept thinking about how cold that water was.

The man and the girl started arguing. I kept one hand on my arm and kept my eyes on the maniac with the knife. Another head popped up from the lifeboat. It was a woman.

The girl looked at me now and spoke in clear English, "Can we trust you?"

I took one look at the man with the knife and a long hard look at the coastline a couple of miles away. "You can trust me. Honest."

She spoke to the man and he seemed to be satisfied. He backed off and kept his hand on the boom so it couldn't smack him in the head. The sail was making an awful noise in the wind with the slack lines. I was afraid it might rip again.

"What's going on?" I asked the girl. She looked like one of the Pakistani kids from my old school. "Who are you?"

"I'm Tamara," she said. "This is my mother and father." The mother nodded. The father looked like he was waiting for a bomb to drop out of the sky.

"I'm Greg."

"And you are bleeding. I am sorry. My father saw your uniform."

"What uniform?" Then I looked down at the colors on the floater jacket. Somebody really out of touch might have considered it a uniform. "I'm not a cop or anything," I said.

"What are you?"

I didn't know what to say. I looked around at the empty ocean, the distant icebergs and the receding coastline. My arm was burning. "I'm someone who wants to help," I said.

"How?" she asked.

"Let's get ashore before we end up in Greenland."

I tied a rope onto the lifeboat. Tamara persuaded her father to change places with her. I didn't trust that knife near all my vital organs. It would be a slow, difficult trip towing that much weight. We would need to tack a bunch of times to get near Deep Cove. But what else was there to do?

It wasn't until we were under sail going a really mean half a mile an hour that I realized I was sharing my Laser with one of the most beautiful girls I'd ever met.

Chapter Four

"We used all of our money to come here on a big ship," Tamara said. "When we came into Canadian waters, the man said we were only a few miles from shore. We got in the life-boat and they lowered us into the water. But there were no oars."

"How long have you been out here?"

"Two days."

"Were you scared?"

"No," she said, looking far off toward the horizon.

"You're lying."

"Maybe," she said, and smiled.

"You're refugees, aren't you?"

Suddenly she looked nervous. "Will you turn us in?"

"What do you mean?"

"Will you turn us in and have us put in jail?"

"No," I said. "It doesn't work that way."

"My father says we must avoid getting caught. He has been told there are very few people living on your coast. He says we can just go ashore and live there. In peace."

I wanted to try to explain a lot of things just then. I wanted to paint a picture for her of the rugged coast of Newfoundland and tell her that you couldn't just live in total isolation, even here.

"In our country there is much fighting and killing. My father was in prison. He would have been executed. He escaped. We found a ship. First to Amsterdam. Now to here. If we can avoid the authorities, we will live again as a family."

"The immigration people will help," I said. "I've heard about stuff like this in the news."

Slowly but surely we were nearing the coastline. But even once we got near shore, it would be another slow four miles along the coast before we would get to Deep Cove. There was nothing but high cliffs and narrow gullies along here. Nowhere to go ashore. And if the wind changed direction we might as well be ten miles back out to sea.

Tamara was looking back at her mother and father. Her mother looked pretty nervous, but her father looked like a volcano about to erupt. I rubbed my arm where I had been cut with the knife. It had stopped bleeding. It stung from getting wet with salt spray, but I knew it wasn't very deep. I'd be okay.

Tamara gave me a soft sad look. "I'm sorry," she said. "My father thought you were going to arrest us."

"Oh yeah, my uniform." I had been so caught up in trying to keep us on course that

I hadn't noticed that Tamara was shivering. With one hand still on the rope and a foot on the tiller, I undid my floater jacket and handed it to her.

She shook her head no.

"Take it. If you fall in, it will float you. Can you swim?"

"A little."

"Yeah, but can you swim in water that just came down from the North Pole?"

"I don't understand."

"Just put on the jacket. Please."

The magic word. She put it on. I showed her how to snap it up. My hand brushed against her long black hair and I found myself looking into her eyes. I guess I forgot I was trying to steer a sailboat just then because I was holding the sail too stiff and we tipped up very high on my side. I had to grab onto Tamara to keep her from sliding out of the boat and giving the floater jacket a real tryout.

When I regained control I apologized. I looked back at her old man and gave him the thumbs-up. I don't think he understood.

That's when I saw the Coast Guard ship headed our way. "Look," I told Tamara. "We're in luck. If I can signal them somehow, you guys will be safe and sound in no time. They can see my sail, I'm sure, but they're too far out to see much else. They have no reason to think we need help."

I was thinking that maybe I could flap the sail in some erratic manner and then they'd notice and come check us out.

Tamara was looking back at her father. He saw the boat too and was shaking his head sideways. The knife was back in his hand. "What's wrong?" I asked her.

"Do not signal them. They will send us back."

"No, they won't. I promise. It's not like that."

"You don't know. They have guns, right?"

"Well, I don't know. Maybe. But look, it's just the Coast Guard. They're out here to help."

"No!" her old man shouted at me from behind. He said something to his daughter in a rapid rattle of language.

"We must hide," she told me. "My mother and father are very afraid. We need your help. We must trust you."

"Where are we going to hide out here?" I asked her. This all seemed crazy. I looked at the steep cliffs along the shore. We were already in much closer than I liked to be. With the wrong gust of wind we'd be chewed up by granite. "There's nothing I can do."

"There," Tamara said, pointing to a narrow gully that cut from the sea into the sheer rock face. It was about twelve feet wide.

"You can't just pull into a little inlet like that with a sailboat. There are a lot of factors to consider here." I suddenly sounded like somebody else. I realized that I sounded like my father. He was always the one who would tell me to look at a problem logically. Logic told me that I couldn't slip my Laser between those two big rocks like it was a quarter dropping into a video game.

"I can't get in there," I repeated. I saw the Coast Guard cutter was headed our way now. It was getting closer. I wanted to tell Tamara that they'd never come in this close to shore anyway, so don't worry.

But she was already pulling on the rope that tied us to the lifeboat. She was about to get back in with her parents. Her old man would cut the rope and they'd take their chances without me.

"Tamara," I shouted to her, pulling her back. I realized that, this time, the logical thing to do might not be the right thing to do. "Stay put. Tell your father we're going in. They'll never find us in there."

Tamara gave me a puzzled look but ducked beneath the sail and sat back down. "You said you can't get in there."

I checked the wind. Light onshore. I tried to get a good look at what was beyond the narrow channel, but I couldn't see a thing from this angle.

Tamara's father now was shouting something at me. He was pointing his finger towards the narrow passage.

"Okay, okay," I said. I shoved hard on the tiller and lined us up perfectly. The wind was directly behind me now and it would be a fast downwind run straight in. The rope towing the lifeboat pulled taut. The weight of the other boat acted as an anchor brake at first, but then, as the sail filled out, we started to pick up speed. I lay down low to see under the sail.

Then walls of dark rock swallowed us up. The aluminum boom banged hard against a rock and sent off an eerie sound like a Sunday morning church bell. I jammed the tiller hard left to avoid a submerged rock and then back to get us on course. On course to where? I kept wondering.

And as suddenly as we had entered the gully, we were beyond it and back in the sunshine. We were in a small protected harbor. Up ahead was a tiny beach of stones. High, barren hills surrounded us on all sides, and a long thin waterfall splashed down right into the seawater.

I aimed straight for the beach of black pebbles, raised the centerboard and drove us right up onto dry land. I hopped out and pulled the lifeboat in behind me.

Tamara and her parents looked around in wonder.

"Welcome to Newfoundland," I said.

Chapter Five

Tamara's mother jumped onto the beach and fell to her knees. She bowed her head. Maybe she was praying. Tamara went over to her. I guess the woman thought she was never going to set foot on solid ground again. Meanwhile, Tamara's father was gathering a couple of sacks from the boat. He seemed anxious to get out of here. The knife was still in his hand as he lifted his wife up off the stones and began to bully her towards a small trail that led inland.

I ran to Tamara as they started to hurry off. "Where are you going? You can't just go wandering off into the wilderness. You don't know anything about this place. You could die out there."

Tamara didn't look at me. "We could have died out on the sea, but we didn't. Now we have safely arrived and we are free. I thank you. Now you must leave us alone and tell no one we are here."

I didn't know what to do. I stood there trying to figure these people out. What could I do? Just let them wander off, maybe to starve or fall off a cliff or something? Or what if I went home and phoned the police to come find them? Then what? Tamara's father would go at them with a knife and he would get thrown in jail. They might all get sent back. There were no happy endings.

I heard my father's voice. *Just be reasonable. Think through all the options.* As far as I figured I had just one option: trust.

"Tamara," I shouted. She turned around. "You have to trust me. If you don't come with me, your whole family will be in big trouble. I'll take you to my house. It will be warm. There will be food. We'll take care of you."

But it wasn't enough. They were having a hard time scrambling up the steep path, but these were stubborn, desperate people. They'd make it out of here, but where would they be then?

"You can hide at my house," I said finally. "My mom and I will hide you and tell no one until you have a safe place to go to. Trust me."

They stopped. Tamara was speaking to her father and mother. They were arguing. I didn't take a step towards them. Her father was glaring at me with mistrust. I rubbed my arm. Silently, I let go a little prayer of my own. All my life I had been doing everything for me. The sailing, the competitions, the glory. But nothing ever felt quite like this. These people needed me. I could help them and no one else could. And I guess I needed them too.

The parents were still arguing. As far as I could tell, the mother wanted to trust me but the father didn't trust anyone anywhere. He would get his way, I was certain. He was the boss. Tamara was talking too, but they were ignoring her. She was getting mad.

Then Tamara stopped arguing. She looked back at me. I hadn't moved. *Trust me*, I said silently over and over in my head. *Please let me help.*

Tamara walked away from her parents and back down the slope towards me. Her eyes were fixed on mine. Her father started to yell something at her, but she didn't turn around. She walked straight up to me and took my hand, then turned around and looked at her parents.

It was pretty rough going to get back to Deep Cove. We hiked over some of the wildest country I had ever seen. I managed to keep my bearings as long as I knew where the sea was. Tamara and I talked the whole way. I didn't let go of her hand, not even once. Her parents remained silent and followed closely behind us.

I took the back way through the berry fields to get to my house. That way we could walk pretty well right up to the door without anyone seeing us. It was near dark when we got there. Boy, was I hungry, but Tamara and her family must have been much worse off.

When I got to the door, I was pretty nervous. How was I going to explain this to my mom? I decided to knock.

She opened the door and blinked.

"I invited some people over for supper," I said matter-of-factly. "They're new in town."

"Hello. Pleased to meet you," Tamara said.

My mother saw the blood on my sleeve. It looked worse than it actually was. "What happened to you?"

"I cut it on a sharp rock. It's nothing. Can we come in?"

My mother said nothing but stepped aside. We entered in a silent parade. Before we all settled down in the living room, Tamara's father whispered something to her. In a low voice she said to me, "Do not tell her who we are. Just say we are friends."

Do you know how hard it is to keep secrets from my mother? I wanted to say. Besides, they didn't look like anyone from Newfoundland.

Dinner was haddock and potatoes and a huge salad. After the food was set on the table, my mother grabbed me by the arm and pulled me into the kitchen. She was furious with me for not explaining what was going on.

"Who are these people?" she demanded. "I don't trust that man. I don't like any of this. What are they, drug smugglers?"

"Just relax, Mom. I had to promise them I wouldn't tell you who they are."

My mom folded her arms. "That's a promise you're going to have to break, buster. Those people are sitting at our table. They're eating our food. I want to know who they are."

I tried to think what my father would do. I didn't think he'd ever been in a situation like this.

Chapter Six

"They're refugees. They won't say where they're from. They want to live in Canada. They want to live *here*. I found them drifting around off the coast in a boat. We need to help them, but Tamara's father doesn't trust anybody."

"Who is Tamara?" my mother demanded.

"Tamara's the girl," I said. "She's really something. I like her a lot."

My mother looked at the way I was smiling. Then she threw up her hands and talked to the ceiling. "My son has a crush on a girl he just found in a lifeboat. What next?"

"Quiet," I whispered. "They might hear. Besides, I just met her. I don't have a crush on her."

"We need to sort this out rationally," my mother said, talking like my father now. "We need to call the immigration people in St. John's right away. They'll know what we should do." She picked up the phone and dialed 411 for information.

"No, we can't!" I told her in a loud whisper. I took the phone from her and hung it up.

"Why?" my mom wanted to know. She didn't like the way I was acting.

"Because Tamara's father is afraid of cops, of anybody in authority. I promised we wouldn't turn them in."

"Promised? Are you crazy? If we don't turn them over, we'll be breaking the law."

I shrugged. "They need our help. Now let's eat supper like everything is normal."

"Normal?" she repeated, as if she'd never heard the word before. But before we could return to the dining room, we heard the front door open.

My mom looked at me. "Oh, no. There's more of them."

"No, I don't think so."

We rushed out of the kitchen. It was Harold.

"Oh, boy," I gasped. Tamara's father had jumped up and pulled out his knife. He had Harold pinned up against the wall with the knife poised near the old guy's stomach.

Harold's eyes were bugging out of his head and he had his hands thrown back. Mom screamed. Tamara's mother was jumping up and down.

"Just everybody relax," I said, sucking in my breath. "Tamara, tell your father this man is my friend. He's not from the police. He's just a friend."

She translated.

Tamara's father was slow to be convinced.

"His name is Harold," I told her father. "He's a nice guy. Don't kill him."

Although the tension didn't drain from his face, Tamara's father lowered the knife.

Harold spoke gently to the man who had been about to slice his belly. "That looks like a good knife. Had one like it once that I used to gut mackerel with. Lost it in a squall. Always liked that knife."

"That does it," my mother said, regaining her courage. "I want all these people out of my house," she told me. "No ifs, ands or buts."

Tamara's family understood without translation. My mother was pointing toward the door. Tamara's father looked a little hurt. Her mother just hung her head low and sobbed. They were picking up their few bags when Harold cleared his throat. He understood perfectly who these folks were.

"Now wait a minute," he said to my mom. "I think we just had a little misunderstanding. Like you kept trying to tell me, I should knock before I come in. Hard to teach an old dog new tricks. It was my mistake. He probably thought I was some kind of prowler."

"He thought you were a cop," I corrected.

Harold laughed. "I assure you, I'm no cop. In fact, the Mounties still haven't forgiven me for smuggling a little rum way back when."

"Out!" My mother repeated. "You too, Harold. Get out!"

Harold scratched his head.

I walked over to Tamara. "Mom, you can't ask them to leave. I promised they could stay here. For the night at least."

"I don't trust him," my mother said, pointing to Tamara's father. "I don't trust him and that knife."

I let go of Tamara's hand and walked over to her old man. I held out my hand and pointed to the blade. Tamara said something to him. Suddenly he pulled the knife out of the sheath again.

My lungs stopped working and my heart went on strike. But then he placed the knife gently in my hand. "Sorry," he said in English. "Sorry."

And so we all sat down to dinner, Harold included. We were all nervous and uncomfortable. Harold said it was just about the best fish he'd ever seen a mainlander cook.

My mother looked at me. "Greg, I wish your father was still around for this."

"Me too," I said.

Chapter Seven

People who live in Newfoundland outports have a curious ability to ignore the rest of the world. On top of that, nothing seems to come as a shock to them. Nobody seemed to think it unusual that a refugee family from Southeast Asia had found its way by boat to Deep Cove and that they were living with a mother and son from Toronto.

"We've seen all kinds of trouble here,

Greg," Harold explained to me. "We don't give anyone a hard time who wants to be here. Just like you and your mom couldn't kick out these lost souls."

All kinds of clothing and food started pouring into the house from the thirty or so families around the cove. After a few days, it felt like we were all part of some big happy family.

Tamara's father seemed less uptight. I showed him how to split wood for the wood stove. And Tamara's mother liked to help out with the washing and cooking.

After breakfast one morning, Mom took me for a walk out back to the stream. "This is crazy, you know. These people can't just stay here."

"Why not?" I asked. I had spent some time walking in the hills with Tamara. I had even taken her for a sail in the cove, after retrieving my Laser from down the shore. I felt I was just getting to know her.

"They can't live with us forever."

"There are a few abandoned houses in Deep Cove. They could settle into one."

"They don't have any money, though."

"That doesn't seem to be a big deal here," I said. "There are gardens and there's fish and berries and extra clothes and wood to heat with and everybody around here seems plenty generous — "

"No," my mom interrupted. "That's not it. They are here illegally. We don't know the whole story. Immigration will find out sooner or later. Things could get very messy."

"Yeah," I said. "But we can't just turn them over. They could get shipped back. I couldn't let that happen. Besides, they're a lot like us."

"How do you mean?"

"I mean they've lost something big in their lives, something important. They're in a new place and cut off from the past. We're refugees too, Mom. We're a lot like they are."

She didn't say anything. The back door opened and Tamara's father came out with an axe. We both watched as he set a chunk of wood on the cutting block and smashed it in half with a crack of the axe blade.

In the middle of summer, Newfoundland could be a surprising place. From the tops of the hills you could still see a few icebergs offshore. But it was warm outside and the air was full of the sweet smells of bayberry and wintergreen. I had stopped thinking about pushing myself to the limit sailing at the speed of light. Instead, I found that I was quite content to go hiking up into the hills and to pick raspberries, strawberries and bake apples with a beautiful Asian girl.

I had forgotten about Toronto, about school, about how much it had hurt to lose my father.

At Tamara's prompting, I took her parents along one morning for a trek to a far-off berry field. Harold had told me about the place. "I promise you, Greg. This is the raspberry mother-lode." He drew me a map.

Tamara's parents loved the hike through the craggy countryside. They had picked up a little English and we could all communicate better. We were on a first-name basis now. Her father's name was Ravi and her mother's name was Indra.

As we were returning home that day, I felt like I had grown to understand them all much better. And I had come to believe what I had first considered impossible. They *had* just arrived on this remote coast and settled in. They were doing great and nobody seemed to mind at all.

But as we came to the top of the hill behind the house, the bad news hit us all at the same time.

There was a police car in our driveway. Two cops and a man in a suit were talking to my mother. I swallowed hard and stared at the scene below. I turned around to assure Tamara's family that they shouldn't worry, that we would help them see it through. They were already scrambling away down the back side of the hill, stumbling over stones and running for their lives.

I sprinted after them. I grabbed Tamara by the arm, spinning her around.

"You betrayed us," she said.

"No. I didn't. I couldn't. And neither could my mother."

Her father was tugging at her to continue. "Leave us," he said to me in English.

"I can't. Please, stay here. You can come back down when they leave."

Ravi put his hands on my shoulders. "You go. Find out. Come back to us. Please."

"You'll stay here?" I asked him. "Promise?"

"Promise," he said.

Chapter Eight

I waited until the cops got back into their car and drove off. Then I skidded down the steep slope and went inside.

My mom was sitting on the sofa wringing her hands.

"They were looking for Tamara's family, weren't they?"

"Yes," she said, not wanting to look at me.

"Well, what did you tell them?"

"I'm not a very convincing liar," she said. "I told them I had never seen any refugees. I don't know if they believed me. Where are they?"

"Up in the fields near the bog. I think they're scared again."

"So am I," she said. "I don't think we can keep this up. That man was from immigration. He's suspicious. We don't know what we've gotten ourselves into."

"But Tamara and her parents are happy here. They are good people. You can see that yourself."

"I know. But we can't hide them from the rest of the world forever."

"Why not?"

"Because I'm a bad liar. And I don't like having to lie. And what about *us*? If we're not careful, we might end up in jail. I should have told the truth. Maybe it would all be very simple. We have no reason to believe they will be made to leave the country."

"I sort of thought that from the begining.

But how are we going to convince Ravi of that?"

"And if we make contact with Immigration, they'll know I already lied and will be wondering why we were trying to cover up for the refugees. We have a problem."

I thought of Tamara and her folks. "I'm going to go up and tell them it's okay to come down now."

"Suppose my acting was so bad that the Mounties are nearby watching?"

"We'll cross that bridge when we come to it." I was thinking just then how much Tamara meant to me. She was unlike any girl I'd ever met in Toronto. She was brave and smart and had those eyes that could see right into me — the real me.

I found the three of them sitting on the top of a bare rock, staring into the sunset.

"We're not going back down with you," Tamara said.

"But they're gone. My mother told them nothing."

"Yes," Ravi said. "But for us . . . danger. You . . . not understand."

"Yes, I do understand," I said.

"We stay," Ravi said and pointed to the spot on which he was sitting.

"Tamara, tell him. This is not necessary."

Tamara looked at me with those big dark eyes. She led me to a ledge and made me sit down with her. We were above a sheer wall of granite that dropped off a hundred feet to the sea. The sun was setting and the world had a warm reddish glow. Gulls swooped below us along the cliffs. This strange feeling came over me. It was the most mixed-up thing that I ever felt. Sitting down with Tamara, I felt like this was the most perfect moment of my life — her, this beautiful place, the huge impossible expanse of the darkening sea beneath us. I wanted it all to stay like this forever.

But then in the backwash of this feeling was something else — it was like a dream about to shatter.

"You go home," she said to me. "We will stay up here for tonight and see what tomorrow brings. My father will not let us go down."

I was afraid I was about to lose her. "You've trusted me and I haven't let you down, have I?"

"No. But we must be very careful."

"You'll be okay, I promise. No one called the police. They were just checking up on people. Nothing's wrong."

"We've told you very little about us," Tamara said, her voice changing. "Now I will tell you something."

I looked down at the gulls swirling in the mist that was now rising from the sea.

"My father was a soldier," Tamara began. "He fought as he was instructed. He burned forests and farmers' fields as he was told. He killed other men. He followed orders very well."

A shudder went through me. "Who was he fighting for? Why?"

"This will sound strange, but that is not

important now. He did not want to do these things. He had been away for one year. We had not seen him at all. Then one day he came home. I did not recognize him. He looked sick. I thought he might die. He had simply stopped being a soldier. My father said he could not kill anyone any more, no matter how many orders they gave him."

"He was a deserter," I said. "That must have taken a lot of courage."

"Yes. But he had no choice. He could do it no longer. He was very sick and could not think well. A week went by and then one night more soldiers came into our house. They dragged my father out. They took him away and threatened to kill my mother and me if we did not get out of the house. When we went outside, they threw gasoline on our house and burned it to the ground.

"We lived in my grandmother's house, not knowing anything about my father until he appeared one night like a ghost — starved, crazy. My grandfather found us a ship to take us out of the country and gave us money.

"Many weeks later, we are here and you find us. We are very far from our home but we must be very careful. My father would kill himself before being sent back. I cannot let that happen."

I felt swallowed up by all the sorrow of their lives. I thought about all the happy, care-free days of my own, sailing around Lake Ontario, while Tamara and her family suf-fered. It almost didn't seem possible. It didn't seem fair. And then my feelings for my own father came back.

"When *my* father died," I told her, "I wondered why there wasn't anything I could do to stop it. I would have done anything to help him, to keep him alive. So I think I un-derstand."

Tamara put her arm around my neck. I leaned over and kissed her for the first time. I felt like one of those gulls below me along the cliffs, just floating through the misty evening sky.

Tamara convinced me they would be okay for one night alone in the wilderness.

They would not let me stay with them, but I did make one more trip to the house and back to bring them food, a tent and warm clothing.

At home in my own bed, I had a hard time sleeping. Tamara's story kept me awake for a long time. I kept wondering if I had done enough to help this family that seemed so strange yet so familiar.

Chapter Nine

I woke not long after dawn with an awful feeling in the pit of my stomach. My first thought was that something had happened to my mother, that someone had taken her away. But it was just a fragment of a nightmare I was having. When I looked in her room, she was still asleep.

I threw on a coat and ran out the door. It was a gray, damp morning and the sky seemed full of ghosts as I climbed the slip-pery path back to where Tamara's family had spent the night. As I got higher up, I broke clear of the fog bank that was hugging the cove and I could see the morning sun break through the clouds higher up . . . a good omen.

But it was not enough. When I reached the place where I had left Tamara's family, they were gone. I frantically raced about, looking for some sign of the direction in which they might have gone, but there was nothing.

A terrifying sense of loss swept over me, a feeling of powerlessness and defeat. I'd like to say I was worried about Tamara's family, that I was feeling bad for them, but it wasn't that at all. I was feeling sorry for myself. I was thinking that I had lost Tamara for good.

There wasn't a clue as to which way to go so I scrambled back down the hillside, slipping, bruising myself on the rocks along the way.

The fog had begun to clear a bit in the cove. From the hill, I saw a car pull up in front of the house. It was white with a light bar on top. The Mounties were back. My mother was right; she was a lousy liar.

I wanted to scream at them — it was all their fault. Why couldn't they just leave people alone?

My feet finally found the gravel drive that led to our house. A cop was standing by the car. He gave me a curious look. But before I could get out a single insult, I was face to face with my mother.

"Greg," she said to me. "Something's come up. Something about some foreigners in a lifeboat." Her acting was bad, real bad. "There's probably some misunderstanding, but this officer says I have to go into St. John's with him. They just want to ask me a few questions."

I looked at the hulking Mountie. He had a gun on and a face like I'd seen on some bad guy in an Arnold Schwarzenegger movie. "You can't do that," I said. That fear of losing my mother crept back into my skull.

"It's just standard procedure," he said in

a voice cold as steel. He held up a piece of paper. "This court document says we can do this."

Things began to blur before my eyes.

"It's okay," my mom said, now sounding a little more like herself. "I'm sure it's all a misunderstanding. I'll be home later today."

The cop walked towards his car and waited for my mom to say goodbye to me.

She gave me a hug and whispered in my ear, "Tell our friends that whatever happens, we'll help them. We won't let them go back. I promise." And then she gently pushed me away and walked to the police car.

I froze on the spot. I couldn't tell her right then that Tamara's family was gone. She'd react and then the Mountie would know they *were* around here somewhere. I watched as the car backed up and drove off. At that moment, I had the feeling that Tamara's father was right. The authorities couldn't be trusted. And it was my fault that my mother was in trouble.

I walked down towards the wharf looking for a friend, looking for Harold. He found me first. He poked his head out from one of the fishing shacks.

"Greggie, saw that Mountie up at your house. You should have sent him down here. Looks like somebody stole old Calvin's dory — oars and all. Not something that usually happens around here. Must've been a tourist. Hard to figure."

I could tell that he thought it was a big joke and that one of the local kids had probably just taken it as a prank. But I knew better.

"When was it taken?"

"Could have been any time last night. Calvin came down to go fishing this morning and nearly fell straight in the drink when he tried to climb into a boat that wasn't there," Harold said. Then his brow wrinkled. "Why?"

"Ravi, Tamara and Indra are gone. They saw the Mounties yesterday. They're scared. Ravi thinks they'll get sent back." I looked out through the channel to the open sea. There were whitecaps out there from a strong easterly breeze coming up. "They're out there somewhere. Even if I could find them, I don't know if I could convince them to come back."

I looked at my little Laser tied to the dock. I let out a sigh. "Well, I guess I better try." I jumped down into the boat and began to undo the rope that kept the sail tightly furled around the mast.

Harold sat and scratched his jaw for a few seconds, then walked over to me. He scrunched down on his haunches to be at eye level. "Not gonna be a good day for sailing, mate," he told me.

"What do you mean?" I asked, lifting the boom into place.

"Look out there. Winds will be up to fifty miles an hour before noon. Big nor'easter. Mean as she gets. Not fit for man nor beast."

"Ravi doesn't know the sea. They'll drown out there." I began to tighten the sail. I dropped the centerboard. "Wanna undo that line back there?" I asked Harold.

Harold just looked at me and held onto the side of the boat. "I'm not gonna let you leave this wharf."

"The hell you're not!" I shouted at him. I was just waiting to get good and angry with somebody. Harold was it. I kicked at his hand. He pulled his arm back and shook his fingers where my boot had connected.

He remained cool. "Let's call the Coast Guard. Maybe they can send a ship by."

"No," I said. "Ravi wouldn't let the Coast Guard take them. He doesn't trust anyone in a uniform. He might rather see his family sunk to the bottom of the sea before they turn themselves in to the authorities. He has good reason not to trust anyone."

Harold shook his head. His eyes were fixed straight on me. "Anyone but you, right?"

"Right," I said, reaching for the mooring rope.

"Wrong," he said. "Anyone but us. Now forget this bathtub toy and get your ass in my boat. We'll find 'em."

Chapter Ten

As we pushed out of the cove into the open sea, the waves began to roll the boat around. Spray splashed over the sides. Harold threw me a jacket. The wind was picking up steadily now as we got further from shore. The waves grew bigger and bigger, some as high as seven and eight feet.

Harold turned west, away from the wind. The boat slid smoothly down the face of a wave. This old fishing tug of his was a big, heavy boat, but it felt like a matchstick in this powerful sea. "Most likely they'd come this way, with the wind. That old boy wouldn't be able to row against a breeze like this. We're far enough out now. I think that if they're anywhere, they'll be between us and the shoreline."

"Anywhere along here is going to be a pretty tough place to go ashore," I reminded him. "I know from experience."

"Join the club," Harold said. "I sank out here once back in 1957. Got caught in a storm that came up out of nowhere. I was in too close and a bloody rock punched a hole in my old crate big enough to let in half the Atlantic Ocean."

The wind was behind us now and we were picking up speed. We were cruising up the back of a wave and then skidding down the front. If I hadn't been so worried about Tamara, I would have called it fun.

"How'd you get in?"

"Well, I had a pile of lumber on board I

was bringing back from the mill. Just tied it up in a bundle, tied myself to it and washed in with the waves."

"You were lucky," I said.

"That's the name of the game."

Right then I was thinking that luck was about all we had going for us. It was a big ocean, an impossible coastline. I guess Ravi was good and scared and wanted to get somewhere far away. He figured that he'd get away quicker in a rowboat. But I'm sure he hadn't been expecting this weather. I kept thinking of Tamara out here somewhere. It made me shiver.

"Only so much luck to go around, though," Harold added. "I've seen it all. Some boys go straight down the first boat they sink. Others get away with it. But around here, in these waters, luck's only good enough to save you once. When the second time comes around, you don't stand a chance. The bloody sea remembers the first time and feels cheated."

"That's ridiculous," I found myself saying.

"That's like some stupid old superstition."

I could tell I'd hit a sore point. Harold frowned. "You grow up around here, you don't call it superstition. You count the men who go out and you count the men who come ashore and you study the facts."

I wanted to debate with the old fart just then, but I knew it wasn't the time or place. I kept my mouth shut and studied the sea.

"Don't worry," Harold said, realizing we shouldn't be arguing about anything. "A kid from Toronto can't drown out here. He'd never let himself die on account of mere superstition."

I thought about my first dunk in the waters here. I thought about the ice — the bergs, the bergers and the cold, cold water. I thought about the fact that Harold saved me the first time I lost it out here. I wondered if I was ready for number two after all.

Harold handed me a beat-up pair of binoculars. "Up periscope," he said. He pointed a finger towards the top of his boat's cabin. "Get up there and look. Just hang on good."

The waves were still getting larger, the wind stronger. I grabbed onto a brass handhold and hoisted myself up on top of the cabin. I looked for something to hold onto and saw a steel pole. At the top of the pole was an antenna.

"I didn't know you had a radio," I shouted down. "Maybe you should call for some more help. This sea looks pretty impossible. We might not find them in time."

Harold yelled back. "Good idea," he said. "I might have thought of it myself except the radio hasn't worked for three years. No back-up. It's just us. Besides, we're running out of time. That storm's gonna be on us soon. Get a look out."

I looked back to the east and saw the dark horizon. I saw the endless lines of waves, pushing our way. Then I put the binoculars to my eyes and began to scan the water. There was a lot of wild water between us and the dark granite cliffs of the Newfoundland coastline.

"Greg," Harold shouted up to me, "you

want to call it quits, you just say the word."

I kept my mouth shut and held the binoculars up tight against my face. I held on
for dear life as the boat rolled and pitched in
the sea.

Chapter Eleven

I caught sight of something halfway between us and the cliffs. "There!" I shouted. Harold turned the boat in the direction I was pointing.

I fell flat onto the top of the cabin and clung to the aerial, praying it was solidly anchored. When I crawled up on my knees again, though, I couldn't see anything. Maybe it had just been some driftwood.

"Hang on, Greg," Harold said. "I saw something too."

It was an up and down fight to make any headway against the waves. I hung onto the antenna pole and stood again. I waited until we were at the peak of a swell and then put the binoculars up to my eyes.

We were closer now. It was a dory, a dory filled to the gunwales with water.

"Hurry!" I screamed.

Harold made the engine roar just as we took the first real smashing impact of a wave breaking over us. I hung on with all my strength. I saw Harold fight the wheel as the wave threatened to spin us about.

"We're getting in too close," he screamed at me. "Too shallow. We can't take too many like that." Harold was scared.

I heard the engine sputter like it was going to stall, but then it came back to life. Harold gunned it again. I could see the dory clearly now. It was upright but swamped. Still hanging on inside it, though, were three people. I saw Tamara put one arm up in the air and wave.

Their boat was drifting dangerously near the cliffs. At the foot of the cliffs, monster waves smashed on jagged rocks. The wind and waves were pushing the dory closer to the cliffs, closer to disaster. It would only be a matter of minutes. There was no place for them to scramble ashore. There was no way they would get out of there alive.

Suddenly Harold's boat connected with something hard. We lurched to a near stop and I slid across the cabin roof on my stomach. I grabbed onto the steel pole just before I would have ended up in the water.

"That's it," Harold shouted to me as I scrambled off the roof of the cabin. "We have to get out of here. This place is nothing but hungry rocks."

"No!" I shouted. I made him look, made him see Tamara's family.

"Get below and see if we're taking on water," Harold said.

I opened the cabin door and went in. Water was coming in a steady stream through planks that were cracked pretty badly. Already there was a foot of water on the floor. As the boat shuddered and lurched, I made it through the indoor swimming pool and flicked on the bilge pump. If I was lucky, Harold would never notice the noise of the thing.

I clambered back up on deck. "Dry as a desert down there. No problems," I said. I kicked the door shut.

We were off the rock, in one piece, and still floating. Our luck was holding. Harold gunned the engine again between swells and managed to avoid more hidden rocks. In fits and starts we neared the dory.

As we came alongside, I leaned over and grabbed the dory. I tried to hold the two boats together. Ravi grabbed onto the boat as well. We held on grimly as Tamara and Indra climbed across.

Just then a wave crested and cold water smashed down on us like frozen cement. Tamara and her mom had made it in to Harold's boat. The force of the water made Ravi lose his grip. I couldn't hold onto the waterlogged dory. It started to slip away.

The dory tipped and Ravi was thrown out. I looked around for something to throw but everything had been washed overboard.

I watched as Ravi floundered. I tried to use my senses, but nothing made any sense. He was only feet away. There were only seconds before the crest of another wave might push us away from him. I threw myself in the water. It was so cold it felt like hot knives against my arms and legs. I floundered but forced myself to move my arms. Flailing wildly, I grabbed his outstretched hand. I pulled and tugged. Ravi was trying to stay up, trying to swim.

It was like pulling deadweight. I caught a look of terror in his eyes and didn't let myself look again. I swam, I pulled, I cursed the cold. I could see we were sliding up the face of another wave now. I saw the white water near the top. I sucked in a big gulp of air as I saw it coming.

Harold was screaming something at me. Tamara was at the side of the boat. Her arm was reaching out. I locked my hand hard around Ravi's wrist as I felt him start to go under. My other hand shot up like I was trying to dive up into the sky. Tamara grabbed my hand just as the wave smashed down. In the next few seconds of pure fear, panic and hope, I knew that she could not let go. I could not let go. Our whole world depended on us hanging on to each other.

We were on the backside of the wave now. Harold and Indra were pulling Ravi up into the boat. He was coughing and gagging. Tamara pulled me inside and we sat exhausted in the seawater sloshing around on deck. She was still hanging onto me.

Chapter Twelve

I was so cold and exhausted just then that I didn't want to move. I knew we were still in deep trouble. The wind was wailing and the boat was getting battered. Tamara and I were huddled together, which made me think if I was going to die soon, this wouldn't be such a bad way to go. I pressed Tamara tightly against me.

A kick in the ribs brought me back to

reality. Harold's boot had connected with my sense of priorities. "Get up here, Greg, you lazy bum," he snarled. "I need your help if we are going to make it."

I left Tamara and tried to get my footing beside Harold.

"We can't go ashore," Harold told me. "Not for miles in either direction. We don't even have enough fuel to fight this swell all the way back to Deep Cove. Our only chance is to get out to deeper water and go with it, downwind. Ride it out, full tilt."

"I lied about the desert," I confessed. "She's taking water below."

"I know you did. You're like your mother — a bad liar."

"I'll go check on the pump."

"Good idea."

I opened the cabin door. The hum of the bilge pump was music to my ears. The water was still coming in through the seams, but it was only about two feet deep.

"We're okay," I told Harold.

"That's what you think," he countered,

pointing to the maze of frothing waves pounding on exposed rocks straight ahead.

"Get up on top and help me steer us out of here."

"Aye, aye, captain," I said with as much enthusiasm as I could muster.

There were only three major obstacles in our way, but each low island of submerged rock looked deadlier than the one before. Harold tried to use the deeper water of an approaching wave to sneak over top of the first shelf of rock. That put us dead on course for number two. Harold was forced to come about and crawl up the face of the sea demon at full throttle. I held my breath as we reached the peak of the huge swell. The engine sputtered. I thought for a second we'd slide backwards down into the trough right on top of rock number two. But the wave passed beneath us without breaking and Harold pulled back around.

I screamed out, "Hard right!" Harold responded and we barely skirted the third shoal. We had our back to the wind and waves, and even though the storm raged all around, we were suddenly okay. Harold was in control. We were away from the rocks and in deep water.

"You can only fight a storm like this for so long," Harold said as I climbed back down. "Then you have to learn to ride it out. Harrington Cove is up there somewhere. Deep water the whole way."

A few minutes ago, everything had seemed like chaos. Now we were going west, with the wind. I could see there was an awesome order to the sea and the storm. A minute ago they were trying to rip us apart. Now we were skidding along at an amazing speed — engine, waves, wind all working for us.

The sky cut loose with a cold pelting rain. I helped Tamara and her family down into the cabin. Tamara's father still had a troubled look about him. "It's okay now," I told him.

He took his finger and traced across my arm where he had first sliced me with his knife. "Sorry," he said.

"Forget it," I told him. "It was an honest mistake."

We rounded a low headland and Harold eased the boat into Harrington Cove. Finally we were protected from the worst of the storm. When we got to the wharf, we tied up the battered boat and Harold went looking for his cousin, Russell. Russell took us home, got us some dry clothes, a couple of gallons of tea and chowder, and then drove us around to Deep Cove. He never once asked about Tamara and her family.

After all that we'd been through, it seemed strange to be home, safe and sound, long before my mother came back from St. John's.

Then a strange car pulled up.

"Should we hide?" Tamara asked.

"No," I said.

But when the door opened and my mom walked in with the guy from immigration, I had second thoughts.

"Don't anyone move," the man said, dropping his briefcase and holding out his hands, "until I have a chance to explain. My name is Wilkins. I'm with the Department of Immigration."

I looked at my mom like she was some kind of traitor. I went and sat down beside Tamara.

Wilkins took off his coat and sat on a wooden chair. He started to open his brief-case as he began to speak, but my mother stopped him.

"There have been others," she said, speaking directly to Tamara. "The govern-ment is aware of who you are. No one wants to send you back."

She sat silently as Tamara translated to be sure her parents understood.

Wilkins shuffled some papers in his brief-case. "I can't officially say that you have refugee status, but if you are who you say you are, we already know your situation. We can do the first step of processing you in St. John's tomorrow. Then we will put you on a plane to Toronto. There you can join other people from your country who can sponsor you. You need a sponsor to look out for your financial needs."

Tamara translated again. But I could tell she didn't like what she was saying. They seemed to be arguing. Something was still wrong.

Then Tamara spoke up. She seemed very nervous now. "We want to stay here."

"In Deep Cove?" The man seemed flabbergasted.

"In Deep Cove," she repeated. Her father nodded.

"We have standard procedures . . ." Wilkins began. Before he could get another word out, the door flew open. In walked Harold, who had obviously been listening at the door.

"The hell with standard procedures," he told Wilkins. "If they want to stay, let 'em stay."

Wilkins looked up, a bit startled by this wild-haired old rum smuggler. "Who are you?" he asked.

"It don't matter who I am," he said.

"No, it certainly doesn't." Mr. Immigration turned back to my mother as if she would support him. "What I'm offering these people is a chance to move to a city where there is opportunity. Where they can be with others from their country. And, of course, there is also a matter of financial support."

"I don't understand," my mother said.

"Money," Wilkins said, rubbing his thumb and index finger together. "If these people want to stay, they need sponsors. People who will provide money and support while they get on their feet. We can connect them with such organizations in Toronto." He said it as if we'd all understand right away. The bottom line was money.

"We can sponsor them," I said, looking at my mother. "We can support them." But I knew that my mom was just about broke. We'd spent most of the money we had on the house. Dad's life insurance was barely enough to live on.

Wilkins looked around at our humble

surroundings. "I don't think that is possible," he said, almost laughing. "I think you are all being unreasonable. Our studies indicate that a large urban center is the best place for Asian immigrants.

"What would you have if you stayed here?" he asked of Tamara. She translated.

Her father got up and walked up to the man. For a second I thought he was going to pull out his knife again. Instead, he said, "Friends. We have friends here." His English was perfectly clear.

"Look outside," Harold said. We all got up to look.

The drenching rain had finally stopped. The wind was easing. The gravel road up to our place was crowded with people. Everyone in Deep Cove must have been out there on the road. As we looked, they all began to swing flashlights so that lights danced off the dark night sky.

Wilkins didn't quite know what to make of this. He folded his papers back into his briefcase. "I think I'll just head on back to the city. You'll have a chance to reconsider this. Perhaps things will look different to you in a day or so."

"Thank you," Tamara said, this time looking at me. "But I think we will always feel the same." Wilkins shrugged and closed the door behind him. He had to ask people to move aside so he could get to his car and drive away.

Ten months have gone by since then. We survived a long, hard winter. There was a house to be fixed up for the new family of Deep Cove. Everyone in town pitched in to make it livable. It turned out Ravi had a way with wood and he proved to be a very good carpenter. With the leftover lumber he has started to make furniture. There has even been some interest in his delicate chairs and tables from the mainland.

Today I am getting my Laser ready for the first sail of the season. Tamara will be coming along. It's warm for a change and the sun is out. My boat always makes me think of my father. The pain never really goes away. You just learn to live with it.

But when I spot Tamara, making her way down to the boat launch, the pain starts to fade. My father always told me to trust my instincts. And that is what I did when I first came upon Tamara and her family on the open ocean. I *knew* what I had to do. I think that decision was a gift from my father.

It's a lot like sailing. There is no such thing as a straight path to a destination. You have to tack — back and forth — working the wind for all it's worth. And watching Tamara walk towards me, I already feel like I'm flying over the waves, leaning far over the side. The sail is full, stretched tight. And all I have to do is hang on tight and remember what my father taught me — never fight against the wind. Find its strength and make it work for you.

orca soundings

Available now!

Death Wind
William Bell

Allie's life has taken a turn for the worse —
her parents fight all the time and she thinks
she is pregnant. Unable to face her parents,
she runs away. She hooks up with her old
friend Razz, a professional skateboarder, and
goes on the road — right into the path of a
fierce tornado. To survive in the horror and
destruction that follow the storm, Allie has
to call on an inner strength she didn't know
she had.

William Bell is the bestselling author of a
number of teen novels. A former teacher,
William Bell lives in Orillia, Ontario.

orca soundings

Available now!

Sticks and Stones
Beth Goobie

Jujube is thrilled when Brent asks her out. She is not so happy when the rumors start flying at school. Pretty soon her name is showing up on bathroom walls and everyone is snickering and sniping. Deciding that someone has to take a stand, Jujube gathers all the other girls who are labeled sluts – and worse — and tries to impress on her fellow students the damage that can be done by assigning a label that reduces a person to an object.

Beth Goobie is an award-winning author of a number of books for teens. Her most recent book, *Before Wings*, won the CLA YA Book Award, was a Governor General's Award nominee, an ALA Best Book nominee and a Teen Top Ten.

orca soundings

Orca Soundings is a new teen fiction series that features realistic teenage characters in stories that focus on contemporary situations and problems.

Soundings are short, thematic novels ideal for class or independent reading. Written by such stalwart teen authors as William Bell, Sheree Fitch and Beth Goobie, there will be between eight and ten new titles a year.

For more information on the Orca Soundings series or other Orca titles, please call Orca Book Publishers at 1-800-210-5277.

LEXILE LEVEL: 550L
A.R. POINTS: 2.0
A.R. LEVEL: 3.8